Rapunzel's Tale

A STEPPING STONE BOOK™

Random House 🏠 New York

ISBN: 978-0-7364-2680-0 (trade)
ISBN: 978-0-7364-8083-3 (lib. bdg.)

www.randomhouse.com/kids

SteppingStonesBooks.com

Printed in the United States of America

10 9 8 7 6 5 4 3 2 1

Tangled

Rapunzel's Tale

Adapted by
Barbara Bazaldua

Illustrated by
Dave Gilson and Jean-Paul Orpiñas

PROLOGUE

*O*nce upon a time, a drop of sunlight fell from the heavens. From this small drop a magical golden flower sprouted. The Golden Flower had the power to heal. But only one person—a selfish old woman named Mother Gothel—knew where the magical flower grew. Greedily, she kept it secret, for its magic gave her youth and beauty far beyond her years.

Centuries passed, and a glorious kingdom was built nearby.

And then something terrible happened. The pregnant queen fell ill. Determined to save her, the people of the kingdom searched far and wide— until, at last, they found the magical flower.

Seething with rage, Mother Gothel watched from her hiding place as the royal guards uprooted the flower and hurried back to the palace. They created a potion from the flower, and the King fed it to the Queen. The Queen recovered . . . and soon afterward, a tiny golden-haired princess was born.

To celebrate, the King and Queen launched a flying lantern into the night sky. But soon after, on a particularly dark night, a vengeful Mother Gothel crept into the royal nursery, hovered over the royal cradle, and stroked the babe's golden curls as she hummed a lullaby. . . .

Mother Gothel's old and wrinkled hands turned smooth and young again! The flower's healing magic had passed into the tiny princess's hair and was awakened by Mother Gothel's quiet singing.

Quickly, the evil woman snipped a lock of the hair to take with her. But to her horror, it turned brown and lost its power. On the babe's head, a dull tuft of hair remained. The child's golden hair only held its magic when it grew on her head, uncut.

So Mother Gothel stole the tiny princess and took her far, far away to a lonely tower deep in a hidden valley. There the greedy woman raised Rapunzel as her own daughter, never allowing her to leave the tower.

I am Rapunzel. This is my story.

CHAPTER 1

Have you ever had a really big dream? I have. And I discovered that making a dream come true is both hard and wonderful. And when it's over—when your dream has come true—you can find a new one! Somebody told me that once.

My first big dream started as far back as I could remember. Every year, on my birthday, the distant sky outside my tower window would fill with beautiful lights that drifted toward the stars. They were magical and mysterious. And I felt almost as if they were calling, *Rapunzel, come and see us!*

I dreamed that one day I would leave my tower just for one night and go to see the lights up close. Just one night. You see, I had never left the tower where Mother and I lived. It was the only world I knew. Mother said my magical hair was a gift that had to be protected. She warned me that the world was full of dangerous people who would try to steal my hair for its healing powers. That was why I had to stay way up in the highest part of our tower, where she could keep me safe.

Of course, I believed her. She was my mother. I knew she wanted to protect me. And she was wiser about the world than I was. She knew what was right. But with all my heart, I wanted to see those lights. As I grew older, it was all I dreamed about.

So when I woke on the day before my eighteenth birthday, I was determined to ask Mother to take me to see the lights. I felt excited and hopeful—and a little nervous—about asking. Meanwhile, I had two long days before my birthday night.

"What shall we do today?" I asked Pascal, my chameleon friend. He pointed his tail at the window as if telling me to leave the tower. I laughed. Pascal was my only companion, except for Mother, and he could always make me smile.

"Oh, come on, Pascal," I said. "It's not that bad."

It wasn't as if I was bored, living in the tower. I had lots to keep me busy. Every day, I did my chores. Then I read one or all of my three books. I played the guitar, knitted, cooked lunch, played darts, sculpted pots, and made candles. Of course, there was always my hair to brush . . . and brush . . . and brush. Did I mention that my hair was long? My hair was really, really long. I'd never had even a trim. Mother said if I ever cut it, it would lose its magic forever.

But what I loved to do best was paint. My tower walls were covered with my art. My favorite painting was of the sparkling lights. On the day before my eighteenth birthday, I added a picture of myself . . . outside the tower . . . watching the lights. I gazed at my painting and made a silent wish: *Let me be brave enough to ask Mother to see the lights.*

"Rapunzel! Let down your hair!" Mother

Gothel called from the base of the tower. She had come home.

Pascal puffed up his chest and gave me a "be strong" look.

"Rapunzel!" Mother shouted, her voice filled with impatience.

Quickly, I looped my long hair around a hook, lowered it, and pulled Mother up to the window at the top of the tower.

I took a deep breath and crossed my fingers behind my back. "Mother," I said, "for this birthday, I want to see the floating lights."

"Oh, you mean the stars," she replied, admiring herself in the mirror. Mother really did like admiring herself in that mirror. But I knew that I had to speak fast. If she saw the smallest wrinkle, I would be called upon to let her sing the lullaby that made my hair glow. When it glowed, it became magic, and that magic kept Mother looking young and beautiful.

So I told her that I didn't think the

lights were stars. I had charted stars, and I knew they were different from these lights that floated upward and disappeared within a single night.

"These lights only appear on my birthday." I was almost shaking. "I feel as if they're meant for me. I need to see them. I have to know what they are!" *Please, oh, please say yes,* I thought.

But Mother shook her head. "The world is too scary," she replied.

I felt my hopes and my heart sink.

On and on she went, telling me of the dangers outside the tower. I could almost feel ruffians and thugs with fierce faces and pointy teeth creeping up on me. My courage crumbled, and I rushed into her arms, where I felt safe, and she held me tightly.

"Don't ever ask me to leave this tower again," Mother commanded sternly. She stroked my hair with a gentle touch. But her voice held that stone-cold tone I had heard all too many times. I felt myself wanting to

cry from disappointment.

"I love you very much, dear," Mother said as she prepared to leave once again.

"I love you more," I replied.

"I love you most," Mother answered as I lowered her from the window and watched her disappear into the forest. Pascal tried to cheer me up, but the shine had gone from the day. *I have Mother's love. It should be enough,* I told myself. *But all I want is to leave the tower for one day. How dangerous can that be?*

Chapter 2

I didn't know that someone was out there who would change everything.

His name was Flynn Rider, and he was a thief and an outlaw. As I was staring out my window, he and the Stabbington brothers, a pair of cutthroats, were racing through the forest. The mounted palace guards were in hot pursuit. Flynn and the brothers seemed to be getting away—until they reached the end of a deep ravine. There was only one way out—up.

"Okay, give me a boost," Flynn told the Stabbingtons. "Then I'll pull you out."

"Give us the satchel first," they said. Reluctantly, Flynn handed over the satchel with the stolen goods. But as the brothers boosted him up, he snatched it back, unnoticed. The moment he reached the top of the ravine, he dashed off, leaving the Stabbingtons behind. Flynn knew they were too dangerous to trust. This was his chance to get away from them!

Flynn ran through the forest. The palace guards' arrows zinged overhead as he vaulted over low branches, dodged bushes, and darted around trees. At last, he managed to escape all the guards except one: the captain. But the captain wasn't the most frightening. That was his horse, Maximus. Maximus was fast, smart . . . and determined to get the satchel and Flynn Ryder with it.

Neighing furiously, Maximus charged after Flynn. Flynn dodged and ducked and leaped. Maximus dodged and ducked and leaped. Wherever Flynn went, Maximus followed. There seemed to be no way Flynn could escape.

Thinking fast, Flynn grabbed a vine, swung around, knocked the captain from the saddle, and landed on Maximus's back. Maximus dug in his hooves and screeched to a stop. Flynn urged Maximus to run, but

Maximus refused. Eyes blazing, the horse twisted his head around and tried to sink his teeth into the satchel. Flynn held it out of reach, but Maximus kept circling and snapping at it relentlessly.

Astonished by this utterly insane horse, Flynn gave a mighty pull. The satchel flew high into the air, arcing until . . .

. . . it snagged on the branch of a tree hanging over a deep chasm. Flynn sprang forward and began to crawl along the underside of the tree, thinking he could escape the horse. But Maximus followed, prancing along the top of the narrow trunk, stomping his hooves to try to smash Flynn's fingers. With a mighty stretch, Flynn finally grasped the satchel.

There was a loud crack. The tree's roots tore free from the cliff. Flynn screamed and Maximus neighed as they both fell. They hit the bottom of the ravine in a rattling shower of dirt, rock, and broken branches.

As the dust cleared, Flynn scrambled to his feet and slipped into some bushes to hide. To his surprise, he backed into a small cave. Maximus trotted to and fro, sniffing Flynn's trail. Flynn crawled deeper into the cave, toward a pale light glimmering on the other side—an exit! Flynn cautiously stepped outside . . .

. . . and there before him lay a secret valley walled in by sheer, sun-speckled cliffs that protected a lush green oasis. In the distance, a misty rainbow hovered around a tall, glimmering waterfall, which plunged into a beautiful rocky creek. Wildflowers spangled the valley floor. And in the center stood my tower, its creamy stones partly shadowed in the warm light.

Flynn thought all he had to do was climb into the tower and hide out with his satchel for a while, and his troubles would be over.

He wasn't expecting me.

CHAPTER 3

I saw him coming.

As the dangerous ruffian clambered through the window, I was waiting. I bonked him on the head with a frying pan. He slumped like a sack of flour. For a moment, I just stared at him lying facedown on my floor.

I did it! I thought in amazement. *I saved myself from a thug.*

Suddenly, I felt myself overcome with curiosity. Did this ruffian have an ugly, fierce face and pointy teeth, as Mother said they all did? Gingerly, I turned him over and studied him.

His teeth looked just like mine. And his face was not at all what Mother had described. It was, well, nice.

But nice-looking face or not, I couldn't leave him sprawled in the middle of the floor. What if he woke up and came after my hair? I glanced at Pascal, who shrugged. He didn't know what to do, either. Having an unconscious ruffian in our tower was a first for both of us.

Then I thought of my closet. Perfect. I would lock the ruffian in there until I could show him to Mother. He was as limp as a noodle, but much heavier. It took a lot of pushing, but I finally got him stuffed inside. I shut the closet door and leaned against it, feeling wobbly from the excitement.

"Okay, okay," I said, taking a deep, calming breath. "I've got a person in my closet." Now what? Then, slowly, it dawned on me: I had captured a person! I had proved I could take care of myself. Surely Mother would agree that I was strong enough to leave the tower and go to see the lights.

Just then, I noticed a satchel lying open on the floor. Curious, I reached in and pulled out a golden circle with points on it. I slipped it over my wrist, but it just dangled there. Pascal giggled at me. Then

I put it on my head and stared at myself in the mirror. Seeing myself gave me the strangest feeling. There was something familiar about this golden circle . . . thingy.

Don't be silly, I told myself. *You have never seen anything like this in your life.* Or had I?

"Rapunzel! Let down your hair!" It was Mother, calling from outside.

Quickly, I tucked the golden circle back into the satchel and shoved it out of sight. I didn't want to show it to Mother yet. First, I wanted to surprise her with the man. I smiled as I pictured her telling me I was brave and strong enough to face the world— and the lights!

"I've been thinking a lot about what you said earlier," I told her as she climbed through the window.

"I hope you're not still talking about the stars," Mother said as she crossed the room to admire herself in her mirror. Horrified by what she saw, she dabbed at a few small droplets of sweat.

"Floating lights, and yes, I'm leading up to that," I said quickly. "You think I'm not strong enough to handle myself out there—"

"Oh, darling, I *know* you're not strong enough to handle yourself out there," Mother answered. "Rapunzel, we are done talking about this."

But this time, her response seemed stronger somehow—

Suddenly, she whirled around, eyes blazing. "ENOUGH WITH THE LIGHTS, RAPUNZEL! YOU ARE NOT LEAVING THIS TOWER. EVER!"

I flinched. Never leaving the tower? I had always believed that someday, maybe even years from now . . . when I was older . . . stronger . . . but—*never?*

Just then, something clicked deep inside me. I was going to see the lights, with or without Mother's permission. I would get that man in the closet to help me. And I no longer wanted Mother to know about him. Quietly, I moved away from the closet door.

"All I was going to say, Mother, is that I know what I want for my birthday." I spoke calmly. "The paint made from the white shells you once brought me."

I knew it would take her three days to collect the shells. That gave me three days to have the ruffian guide me to the floating lights and bring me home. I felt a tiny twinge of guilt. But I squashed it. I wanted this. And besides, Mother would never find out about the trip.

CHAPTER 4

After Mother left, I opened the closet door. My ruffian fell out with a thud. Quickly, I tied him to a chair with my hair. I wanted to be sure I could trust him before I freed him. But first, I needed him to wake up, so I could actually talk with him.

Good old Pascal tried to help. He climbed onto the ruffian's shoulder and slapped him across the face with his tail. When that didn't work, Pascal stuck his long tongue in the man's ear and wiggled it.

The strange man woke with a start and struggled to get free. But I am very good at tying knots.

"Who are you and how did you find me?" I raised my frying pan just in case. It was a fine weapon, and I wasn't going to let it go.

"The name's Flynn Rider," he said. "How's your day going?"

He blinked one eye at me. *Was that*

supposed to mean something, or does he just have dust in his eye? I wondered.

"Who else knows my location?" I asked, trying my best to sound strong.

I guess you could say that the ruffian started to reply. But then suddenly he looked panicked, and started twisting around in the chair, searching the room.

"Where's my satchel?" he asked.

Aha! I thought, congratulating myself for hiding the satchel. I could use it to bargain. But first I had to know why he had come here in search of me.

"What do you want with my hair?" I countered.

"Why on earth would I want your hair?" He stared at me, confused. "The only thing I want to do with your hair is get out of it."

That was strange. Mother always said everyone wanted my hair. Everyone. Could she be wrong? Flynn certainly didn't seem to care about it. But could I trust him?

I had no choice. I would start at the

beginning and test him, see what he knew about the lights, see how he reacted to my thoughts—but not my feelings, not yet.

I took a deep breath and pointed to my painting behind the curtains on the wall.

"Do you know what these are?" I asked. Flynn nodded. He didn't even seem surprised! "You mean the lantern thing they do for the Princess?"

Lanterns! Of course! I thought. *I knew they weren't stars.*

Quickly, I turned my attention back to Flynn. He was still looking around for his satchel. He seemed so desperate, I almost felt sorry for him—but not sorry enough to tell him where it was.

I needed this. I needed his help. He was the only person who could help, as far as I knew. So I gathered up some courage: "You will act as my guide, take me to see these lanterns in the kingdom and return me home safely. Then and only then will I return your satchel." I took a breath. "That is my deal."

To my surprise, Flynn refused.

Now what? I thought. I glanced quickly at Pascal, who smacked his tiny fists together in a "be tough" gesture. *Okay, you can do this,* I told myself.

"You can tear this tower apart brick by brick," I said. "But without my help, you will never find your satchel."

Flynn cleared his throat, but he couldn't seem to find his words. I had him! I was the one who knew where the satchel was, after all. The way I figured it, he really only had one choice—to agree with me!

"Fine," he said at last. "I'll take you to see the lanterns."

"Really?" I shouted. I couldn't believe it. My plan had worked! What a fabulous day I was having. I had captured a ruffian, made him agree to a deal—and now I was going to see the lights!

Oh, I'll admit that as I teetered at the window ledge with Pascal, I was nervous. The world looked so enormous. Did I really dare go out there? What if Mother was right, and something really terrible happened to me and my hair?

But then I glanced at my painting of the floating lights, and I realized something. I could go on just dreaming about the lights forever. Or I could be brave enough to take this chance to find my dream once and for all. Flynn climbed down with the help of his arrows. And I rappelled down with my trusty seventy feet of hair. I was finally leaving.

CHAPTER 5

If you haven't lived in a tower all your life, it's hard to imagine how I felt as my bare feet touched the ground for the first time. Ever! I put one foot down, then the other. Then I threw myself on the ground and rolled in the grass. It was soft. It tickled! It smelled green and fresh and . . . and . . . completely wonderful!

"I can't believe I did this! I can't believe I did this!" I shouted. Flynn watched with a puzzled expression. I didn't care. *He probably takes things like grass for granted,* I thought as I followed him through the cave to the outside world.

It was amazing. Incredible. Sunlight poured down through the branches of enormous trees, making their leaves shine like green glass. The sky was so much bigger than it had ever looked from my tower window.

The sunlight striped the path with gold. I leaped in piles of fallen leaves. I climbed trees and swung from vines. I was the happiest girl in the world. Mother had said the world was frightening, but she was wrong. This wasn't scary. It was fun!

We climbed a high, grassy hill that was just asking me to roll down it. So I did, laughing as the sky and grass tumbled around me in a whirl of green and blue.

"I'm never going back!" I shouted. I squished my toes in cool mud and splashed in sparkling streams. I chased butterflies through fields of wildflowers. The world was glorious. The day was glorious. It was my best day ever!

Then I thought about how I had betrayed Mother's trust. I threw myself facedown in the flowers. How could I do this to her? Why was something I wanted so much, something that was making me so happy, also making me so miserable?

"I'm a despicable human being," I sobbed,

my voice muffled by all the flowers.

Flynn watched me. "I can't help but notice—you seem a little at war with yourself," he said at last. "But this is part of growing up. A little rebellion, a little adventure—that's good, healthy even." He sounded so sincere, I felt better. But then he continued. "Does your mother deserve this? No. Would this break her heart? Of course."

Now I felt bad all over again.

"She would be heartbroken," I agreed. "You're right."

"I am right, aren't I?" Flynn heaved a deep, disappointed sigh. "Oh, bother. All right," he said. "I'm letting you out of the deal. Let's turn around and get you home."

He must be right, I thought. He went on, "I get back my satchel, and—"

Then I came to my senses. He wasn't getting out of our deal that easily.

"No," I said. "I am seeing those lanterns."

Flynn's shoulders slumped. "What is it going to take for me to get my satchel back?"

Just take me to see the lights as we agreed, I thought. But before I could say anything, something rustled in the bushes. I grabbed Flynn's arm.

"Is it ruffians?" I whispered. "Thugs? Have they come for me?"

A rabbit jumped out, and I felt my face turn red. "I am a bit jumpy," I admitted, laughing sheepishly. "But I'll be fine."

"Probably best if we avoid ruffians and thugs, though, huh?" Flynn said thoughtfully. Then he unexpectedly changed the subject.

"Are you hungry?" he asked. "I know a great place for lunch."

Suddenly, I realized I was famished! And I had never eaten anywhere but in the tower. This sounded like fun!

"Where?" I asked.

Flynn just grinned. "You'll know it when you smell it," he replied, leading the way through the thick forest.

CHAPTER 6

When I first saw the tavern called the Snuggly Duckling, my heart sank. The roof was caving in. The unpainted walls sagged. It actually seemed crooked, as if it had just sort of grown into the tree where it became thickly lodged. I couldn't help thinking that the place looked as if the only thing holding it up was the tree itself, along with years of grime.

Mother was right after all—the world was an ugly place.

Still, when Flynn held the door open, I gathered up my courage and carefully stepped inside. I took one look and wanted to scream. Instead, I froze in terror.

The dingy room was filled with big, hairy, ferocious-looking ruffians and thugs. And they were all staring at me.

"Do you smell that?" Flynn asked. "Take a deep breath."

I did and almost choked. The place reeked of old rotten cheese, unwashed clothing, and dirty feet.

"To me, it's part man smell, and the other part is really bad man smell," Flynn said as he led me into the room.

I tried to breathe through my mouth as we edged past men in spiked helmets; men in armor; men bristling with arrows, swords, and daggers; men with eye patches and yellow—pointy!—teeth; men with long, tangled beards and mustaches. I was shaking so hard, even the ends of my hair quivered. And when I say the ends of my hair, I really mean all seventy feet!

"You don't look so good," Flynn said, though I hardly heard a word he uttered. "If you can't handle this place, maybe you should be back in your tower."

I nodded, terrified. But just at that very moment, an enormous thug with a hook for a hand slapped a WANTED poster with a picture of Flynn against the grimy door.

"Is this you?" the thug demanded. He stared at the poster, then at Flynn. "It's you, all right," he grunted. "Go find some guards!" he shouted to the others. "That reward's gonna buy me a new hook."

But he wasn't the only one who wanted the reward. Instantly, the room erupted in chaos. Tables and chairs flew overhead. Glasses shattered. Wood splintered.

I wanted to stop them, but I didn't know how. Maybe Flynn had brought me here to trick me into going home, but now he was getting hurt. He didn't deserve that.

Besides, I needed my guide—in one piece! I climbed up on a table.

"PUT HIM DOWN!" I shouted. "I don't know where I am, and I need him to take me to see the lanterns. I've been dreaming about them my entire life! Haven't you ever had a dream?"

The room went silent. Everyone stared at me. The thug with the hook approached me. I raised my frying pan, which I had carried

with me from the tower—just in case.

"I had a dream once," he said softly. I've always wanted to be a concert pianist." Suddenly, every ruffian in the room was joining in, talking about his special dream: finding the right girl, becoming a florist, working as a gourmet chef, learning to be an interior designer, doing puppet shows, collecting unicorn figurines. Flynn said he wanted to settle down by himself on his own private island.

It was amazing. The thugs seemed gentle, even nice. Mother always said that all people were bad . . . all the time. But she was wrong about this, too. Even these fierce-looking men weren't scary. In fact, I liked them. They had wishes, hopes, and dreams. Really, they were just like me.

CHAPTER 7

Unfortunately, I didn't have very long to savor my happy feeling. Just then, the palace guards burst in with Maximus. Flynn groaned when he saw the horse. I thought perhaps he was a dangerous beast. So when Flynn pulled me down behind a counter, I didn't resist. As we crouched there, Flynn groaned again—he had seen two cutthroats dragged in by the guards. They were the Stabbington brothers. They were in chains, but they were focused on tracking down Flynn , too.

Luckily, one of the thugs opened a door in the floor right near us. It was a secret entryway to a tunnel.

"Go live your dream," the thug said. We ducked into the tunnel and hurried along the twisting, turning passageway through an immense cavern. The lantern light threw strange shadows on the walls. It was so quiet, I could hear the soft thud of our footsteps on the stone floor.

Flynn turned to me and cleared his throat. "Uh, thanks for saving me," he said.

"I am sure you would have done the same for me," I answered.

"I wouldn't hold my breath," he muttered, and changed the subject. "So you really want to see those lanterns, huh?"

Suddenly, I found myself telling Flynn everything about the lanterns: how it seemed so special that they always appeared on my birthday; how I always picked the first one to make a wish on; and how they were so beautiful, they almost made my heart hurt.

I stopped, feeling embarrassed. I had never told anyone except Mother how I felt about the lanterns. I waited for Flynn to laugh at me the way she did. Instead, he just asked why I had never gone to see them before.

I hesitated. If I told Flynn I'd never left the tower, would he think I was so weak that he could break our bargain? Would he think I was a foolish girl who couldn't do anything on her own? Could I tell him about my magical hair? Could I trust him? Suddenly, I realized I already did.

Just then, a loud rumble echoed down the tunnel. The floor trembled. Rocks clattered from the ceiling and skittered across our path. The rumble grew louder. We turned and saw Maximus thundering toward us with a stream of guards right behind him. Somehow, they had found the tunnel entrance, too.

"Run!" Flynn shouted.

We raced along the passageway and skidded to a stop at the edge of a huge cliff. We found ourselves inside an enormous cavern. The only way to escape Maximus was to jump out onto pillars that stood hundreds of feet above the ground. We were trapped. Then, just to make matters even worse, Maximus caught up with us and began a fight to capture Flynn. And

when I say "fight," I don't mean your average horse rearing and clobbering the top of Flynn's head with his hooves. No, Maximus got into in a sword fight with Flynn. I know my knowledge of the outside world was limited, but even I found the whole thing rather bizarre.

Flynn did his best. I think his expertise is in evasion, not actually fighting. The problem was, the fight made me realize that we were standing in front of a huge old rickety dam that was holding back a vast amount of water. All the fighting was weakening the dam, and water was beginning to spurt through. Even I—a person who had just ventured out of a tower for the first time ever—knew that the dam was about to burst. Soon our canyon would be filled with water. A lot of it!

That was when I realized that it was up to me to figure a way out.

And I did.

CHAPTER 8

After all those years of pulling Mother Gothel up into the tower, I realized that this was something I could do. Flinging my hair across the deep crevice, I hooked it on an outcropping . . . and swung. Flynn followed when I tossed my hair back to him. And in no time at all, we had put a large distance between ourselves and Maximus.

The horse was furious. Snorting and neighing, he found a board and kicked it. It fell across the divide, landing on the first pillar we had swung to. Now he had a bridge. Unfortunately, he had also done even more harm to the rickety dam.

As Flynn and I made our way down to the bottom of the canyon, we realized that we were really making our way toward what would soon be a raging river. On top of that, the Stabbington brothers were waiting for Flynn at the bottom!

As I made my last swing to touch down on the floor of the canyon, Flynn was busy evading the Stabbingtons. And the water was roaring into the canyon. We barely managed to start running as the rush of water washed away the Stabbingtons, Maximus, and all the guards!

Then Flynn saw something else even worse. The water had toppled a pillar. It was going to squash us!

Flynn and I raced and scrambled toward the safety of a small cave. We made it just in time. The pillar crashed behind us. I looked quickly for Pascal. Luckily, he was okay.

Stones rained down as Flynn, Pascal, and I huddled, waiting until the roar of the avalanche ceased. But now the silence was overwhelming. We had escaped the Stabbingtons, but the water was rising rapidly inside our little cave, and there was no way out.

Frantically, Flynn tried to move the heavy stones, but they wouldn't budge.

The water got so high that we soon found ourselves shoulder-deep, with nothing but rock above our heads. Flynn dove down again and again, looking for another way out. But it was no use.

"It's pitch-black," he said, gasping for air. "I can't see anything."

I should never have left the tower, I thought. I had insisted on seeing the lights. I had dragged poor Flynn into this. Now we were doomed, and it was all my fault.

"I'm so sorry, Flynn," I said tearfully.

"Eugene," he said. "My real name's Eugene Fitzherbert. Someone might as well know."

I guess we all have secrets, I thought. I was glad Flynn had trusted me with his. Now I was certain I could trust him with my own big secret.

"I have magic hair that glows when I sing," I admitted. Then it dawned on me. My hair could help save us.

I began to sing the lullaby that brought the magic in my hair to life. When my hair began to glow, we dove into the water. We were almost out of breath when we saw an opening. Flynn pulled at a boulder with all his might. It loosened, and we flew out of the cavern in a rush of water. We were saved!

Moments later, we climbed out onto a riverbank and collapsed. I breathed in the wonderful air. Have you ever noticed how exciting plain air can be?

"We're alive! I'm alive! Pascal, we are alive!" I exclaimed.

But Flynn—Eugene—whatever-his-name-was—looked as if he was in shock. He kept whispering to Pascal, something about my glowing hair. I could tell he was more freaked out about that than about his escape!

Finally, I turned to Flynn and saw that he had cut his hand badly on one of the rocks in the cave. I wanted to help him. So I said softly, "It doesn't just glow."

CHAPTER 9

But I waited until later to tell Flynn the other secret about my hair. That night, as we warmed ourselves by a small campfire, I worked up the courage to do it. I knew that Flynn's hand needed to be healed. And, of course, my magical glowing hair had the power to do exactly that.

The problem was, even though Flynn had already seen my hair glow, only Mother and I knew about my hair's healing power. It was the most important secret I had. How would Flynn react? Would it just be too much for him to accept? I mean, glowing hair is odd enough. . . .

Slowly and carefully, I did what I had to do. I gently wrapped my hair around Flynn's hand. He watched me with a perplexed and anxious expression. I could tell he was still wary after seeing my hair light up. But Pascal nodded at me, reassuring me that I was making the right choice.

"I've never done this for anyone before," I said cautiously. "You have to promise not to tell anyone. And promise me you'll just stay . . . calm."

"Okay," Flynn agreed, watching me with a strange expression.

This is when he probably begins to shriek or something, I thought. But I had to help him!

Once again, I sang the lullaby. Slowly, my hair began to glow, until it gleamed where it touched Flynn's wound. In a moment, his hand was healed. Not even a scar remained. Flynn stared at his hand, at my hair, then at his hand again.

"That was incredible," he said. "How did you . . . ?"

"I don't know," I told him. "People tried to cut it once. They wanted its power for themselves." I showed him the lock of brown hair at the nape of my neck. "But once it's cut, it loses its power. That's why it has to be protected. That's why Mother never let me . . ." I stopped, but somehow Flynn understood. He finished for me.

"You've never left the tower," he said. "And you're still going back?"

I nodded. All I had wanted was one chance to see the lights. I truly believed I could see the lights and return to the tower contented, though I was beginning to like this world outside . . . and Flynn. As he went to fetch more firewood, I gazed at the fire, feeling its warm glow.

A cloaked figure stepped from the darkness. The firelight cast shadows that distorted a wrinkled, frightening face. Mother! Without my magical hair, she was already growing older.

My breath caught in my throat. "What are you doing here?" I gasped. "How did you find me?"

She smiled coldly. "I just listened for the sound of complete and utter betrayal and followed that," she answered. She grabbed

my arm, certain that I would follow her lead as I always had. "We're going home. Now."

For a moment, I felt ashamed and guilty— but only for a moment. *I only wanted to see the lights,* I thought. *I wouldn't have left the tower on my own if she had agreed to take me in the first place.* As if in a lightning flash, I understood something else. I was no longer afraid to be on my own. *No,* I thought. I was simply not going to give in this time.

"You don't understand. . . ." I hesitated. "I met someone. He likes me."

"Likes you?" Mother laughed. She was mocking me.

My heart pounded. I was standing up to Mother for the first time. I had seen a bit of the world. I knew Flynn. He liked me!

Angrily, she threw Flynn's satchel at me, telling me that the bag and its treasure were all he wanted. Then she slinked back into the forest.

I stared at the satchel, confused. How had she found it? More importantly, I wondered if I should give it to Flynn now—and prove Mother wrong. But what if she was right? I didn't think I could bear to know. Finally, I hid the satchel, and when Flynn returned, I tried to act as if nothing had happened.

The next morning, a loud snort awakened me. I sat up in time to see Maximus dragging Flynn away. I pulled Flynn free (well, actually, his foot slipped out of the boot that was in Maximus's mouth) and stepped between him and the horse.

I think that was the first time I had really looked at Maximus up close. He wasn't a dangerous beast at all! He looked tired, wet, and almost depressed. I felt sorry for him. Sensing that he needed a little sympathy, I started to reason with him.

I nuzzled his chin and stroked his nose gently. He was really a sweet horse.

"Today is the biggest day of my life," I cooed at him. "I need you not to get Flynn arrested. Just give me twenty-four hours, and after that you can chase each other to your hearts' content. Today is my birthday," I added with a smile. "Just so you know."

Maximus glared at Flynn and snorted. Flynn glared at Maximus and humphed. Finally, Maximus put out his hoof, and Flynn shook it.

Just then, I heard bells ringing. I ran to the top of the hill and looked down on the kingdom, sparkling in the morning sun.

My birthday was beginning. That night, I would finally see the floating lights!

CHAPTER 10

Moments later, Flynn lifted me onto Maximus's back. Together we rode into the kingdom. Flags bearing the kingdom's symbol, a golden sun, flew from every window. A small boy handed me one, and I waved it happily. Garlands of flowers decked the shop windows. Music filled the streets and courtyards.

And the people! Who could have imagined there were so many people in the world? (And not one of them looked scary.) I watched them hurry along the cobblestone streets, chatting with one another, smiling, and laughing. They looked so happy! I longed to join them.

There was only one problem: my hair. It dragged behind me, getting stepped on constantly. When I saw some young girls braiding one another's hair, I asked them to help me. Soon my hair was gathered into

a big beautiful braid with colorful flowers.

The day passed like a dream. We strolled along the streets, stopping to eat pastries from a bakery, admiring shops full of everything you can imagine—even frying pans. My favorite was a bookshop with more books than I could read in a lifetime. I tried to look at every one! Flynn took me to a dress shop, where I tried on the most beautiful gown I had ever worn. Flynn's eyes shone when he looked at me. I didn't quite understand, but I felt myself blushing, my cheeks warmed by his smile.

Suddenly, we heard an announcer calling people to gather around a wooden stage. "Today we dance to celebrate our lost princess," the announcer said. "It is a dance of hope, in which partners separate and return to each other—just as one day our princess will return to us."

I barely heard his words. I was staring at a huge mosaic of the King and Queen. The Queen wore a golden circle on her

head. She held a baby girl with shining green eyes. There was something so familiar about that family. . . .

Just then, the music started, and Flynn and I were caught up in the dance. We whirled and bowed, dipped and swayed, now together, now apart. Each time we returned to each other, it was as if we had always danced together.

At last, the sun began to set behind the castle towers. It was time to light the lanterns. The moment I had dreamed about had arrived.

To my surprise, Flynn helped me into a little boat and rowed us into the harbor to get a good view.

There I was. I had dreamed of this moment for eighteen years—and now I had doubts. What if it wasn't as wonderful as I had always imagined it would be? And now that my big dream was finally coming true, what would I have to look forward to? What would happen next, when this was over?

Flynn smiled reassuringly when I told him my fears. "That's the good part," he said. "You get to go find a new dream."

Quietly, I stared down into the water, until I glimpsed the bright reflection of the first lantern rising. Looking up at last, I felt my heart soar with the lantern. I was finally here, and somehow, I knew this was where I belonged.

Soon hundreds of lanterns floated overhead like glowing flowers. I turned to Flynn. He reached behind his seat and held up a lantern—a gift.

At that moment, I knew Mother was wrong. Flynn wasn't with me just because he wanted the satchel. He cared about me. And I cared about him. And I trusted him with all my heart. So I reached behind my own seat and gave the satchel to him.

I wasn't afraid anymore.

Flynn just set the satchel aside. Then, together, we released our lantern. As it soared away, Flynn took my hand in his. I turned toward him, and our eyes met. He bent closer to me. I didn't really know what he was doing, but a strange feeling came over me. I leaned forward, too, as if drawn to him by some invisible force.

CHAPTER 11

Just then, Flynn pulled away and stared at the shore.

"Is everything okay?" I asked.

"Yes, everything's fine. But there's just something I have to take care of," he said. He rowed to shore and grabbed the satchel. Jumping out of the boat, he turned and gave me a little smile. "Wait for me," he said, and disappeared into the darkness.

After a while, I began to wonder if something had happened to him. Had I done something wrong? Then I heard footsteps along the shore and sighed with relief.

"I was starting to think you ran off with the crown and left me!" I joked.

"He did," a rough voice answered. One of the Stabbington brothers, the one without a patch over his eye, emerged from the bushes and pointed to a boat sailing away. Flynn stood at the prow. I called his name as loudly

as I could, but he didn't even turn around.

The Stabbington brother told me that the golden circle thing in his satchel was the lost princess's crown—and that Flynn had traded it for me and my magical hair. In shock, I realized it was the betrayal Mother had always warned me about.

My heart sank. I felt worse than I ever had in my entire life.

"How much do you think people will pay to stay young and healthy forever?" The Stabbingtons chuckled.

I ran. I had no idea where to go, but I ran as fast as I could.

Then, from behind me, I heard a thump, followed by another thump. Then, out of the darkness, Mother emerged and ran to embrace me.

"Oh, my precious girl!" she exclaimed. "Are you all right?"

The unconscious Stabbington brothers lay behind her. Mother had come to save me once again.

"How did you get here?" I asked her. My head seemed to be whirling with confusion.

"I was so worried, I followed you," Mother explained. "I saw them attack you. Now let's go before they wake up."

I looked back at Flynn's boat, growing smaller in the distance. Feeling as if my heart was tearing in two, I ran to Mother. She took me in her arms.

"You were right," I sobbed as she led me into the forest, back to the tower. "I'll never leave you again."

I didn't know that Mother had revealed the secret of my hair to the Stabbingtons so that they would steal me away from Flynn. They had tied Flynn up in the boat so the palace guards would find him. Then Mother made sure the guards found the Stabbingtons, too. Soon they were in jail right next to Flynn.

When the Stabbingtons told Flynn about Mother's betrayal, he realized she would do anything to keep me with her forever. But

Flynn was powerless—he was in prison, and due to hang for his crimes in the morning.

Luckily, Maximus had seen everything that happened. He raced to the Snuggly Duckling to get help.

They say the darkest hour is just before the dawn, and perhaps it's true. Perhaps it's also true that sometimes the most fearsome-looking people can prove to be the most loyal friends. For just when all seemed lost, the thugs and ruffians arrived. They stormed into the prison and freed Flynn. Thinking nothing of their own safety, they planted Flynn on a wheelbarrow and launched him skyward over the heads of the circling guards— aiming him for a perfect landing atop Maximus. For once, it seemed, Flynn was actually humbled.

With Flynn planted squarely on Maximus's back, the unlikely pair galloped away to my rescue.

Chapter 12

Unaware of anything but my own deep sorrow, I followed Mother to the tower—still believing she had protected me, as she had always promised.

I trudged to my room and sat looking at the little flag that bore the kingdom's golden sun symbol. I remembered the moment with Flynn when the little boy had handed it to me, and how happy I had been. Now Pascal moped beside me, turning blue to match my mood. I looked again at my wall, where I had painted all of my dreams. Suddenly I began seeing the flag's pattern everywhere. I had been painting that golden sun my whole life—as if I'd added the shape without even realizing it.

My mind began spinning with memories: how the kingdom sent up the floating lanterns on the birthday of the lost princess—my birthday; the mosaic of the royal family and how familiar the Queen looked, and the baby's deep green eyes—just like mine; the way the lost princess's crown felt as if it belonged on my head.

As the memories fit together like the pieces of a puzzle, I realized the truth.

My heart pounding, I ran downstairs to face Mother.

"I'm the lost princess, aren't I?" I said.

"Why would you ask such a ridiculous question?" Mother replied. But for the first time in my life, I saw fear in her eyes. At that moment, I knew I was right.

But Mother still tried to manipulate me. "Everything I did was to protect you," she lied. "He won't be there for you."

I felt a sudden chill. "What did you do to Flynn?" I demanded.

She shrugged. "He is to be hanged for his crimes," she answered calmly.

Sorrow and pain tore through me. I loved Flynn. And Mother Gothel had destroyed him so she could continue lying to me and using me and my magical hair.

"You were wrong about the world, Mother," I said. "And you were wrong about me." I could feel my cheeks flush with anger.

She reached out as if to stroke my hair. I pushed her hand away.

"I will never let you use my hair again!" I exclaimed. She fell against her beloved mirror. It shattered, and shards flew across the room. Foolishly, I turned away. And in an instant Mother had clamped an iron chain around my legs.

Suddenly, someone outside the tower called my name. "Rapunzel! Rapunzel! Let down your hair!"

Flynn! He was alive. And he had come back for me.

But he was in danger. Before I could warn him, Mother gagged me with a cloth, chained me to the wall, and waited. A knife glimmered in her hand. When Flynn climbed through the window, he looked at me and gasped.

I saw Mother Gothel's knife flash in the darkness, and Flynn recoiled in agony. He slipped to the floor, badly hurt.

Mother turned to me then and began dragging me away. "No!" I shouted. I knew what I had to do. I promised her that I would stay with her forever, but she had to let me save Flynn first. That was my deal.

"No, Rapunzel!" Flynn gasped, his breathing ragged with pain. "Don't do this!"

My future with Mother would be cold and empty. But if I promised her this, at least I would know that Flynn was alive . . . somewhere. I would have promised anything to save him.

Mother unlocked my chain, and I scrambled to kneel beside Flynn. Quickly, I wrapped my hair around him. He shook his head and tried to push my hair away, but I held it close against him.

"If you're okay, I'll be fine," I said, comforting him. But before I could begin to sing, Flynn grasped a shard of the broken mirror. He cut off my hair. All of it. Instantly, it turned brown. The magic was gone.

With a piercing shriek, Mother began to change. Her skin wrinkled, her hair turned white, her hands twisted into withered claws. Growing older . . . and older . . . she lurched wildly across the room and disintegrated into a puff of gray dust. Her cloak floated to the ground like nothing more than a wisp of cold air on a stormy day.

Flynn was growing pale. He smiled weakly as I knelt beside him. "You were my new dream," he said.

"And you were mine," I answered.

His eyes closed. He was gone. He had sacrificed himself to give me my freedom.

Without my magical hair, without Mother Gothel, I could go anywhere and do anything. But it was all meaningless without Flynn. I tried to sing, desperately hoping to find a trace of magic in my hair. But I had nothing left to give.

I bent my head, and a single tear fell on Flynn's face. The spot where it fell began to glow. I watched, barely able to breathe. Hope was growing bright inside me as the magical glow spread over Flynn's face, his hands, his arms. The last of my healing magic was in that single tear.

The color returned to his face. The grip of his hand grew firm again. At last, his eyes flickered open.

"Rapunzel," he whispered. We gazed at each other joyfully. And then I bent close to him, stroking his cheek with my hand as our lips met with a touch as light as the brush of a butterfly's wing. It was the most magical, wonderful moment. It was my first kiss.

Soon, Maximus proudly carried us back to the kingdom. There I was reunited with my real mother and father—the King and Queen. As they embraced me, I felt the love I had never known with Mother Gothel.

The kingdom treated my return as the most wonderful, happy event that could have come to pass. They had waited years for their lost princess. There was a celebration that lasted for days. Even the pub thugs and Flynn were welcomed. I loved every moment of it. I loved meeting the people of the kingdom and sharing in the festivities. My favorite part, of course, was when my parents and I led the launching of thousands of lanterns by everyone in the kingdom.

And after the celebration was over, and a few years had passed, Flynn and I got married.

I had found my true home at last.